The Solo

The Solo

by Kathryn Lasky

illustrations by Bobette McCarthy

MACMILLAN PUBLISHING COMPANY
NEW YORK

MAXWELL MACMILLAN CANADA
TORONTO

MAXWELL MACMILLAN INTERNATIONAL
NEW YORK   OXFORD   SINGAPORE   SYDNEY

Macmillan Publishing Company is part of the
Maxwell Communication Group of Companies.
Macmillan Publishing Company
866 Third Avenue, New York, NY 10022
Maxwell Macmillan Canada, Inc.
1200 Eglinton Avenue East, Suite 200
Don Mills, Ontario M3C 3N1
First edition
Printed in the United States of America

1   3   5   7   9   10   8   6   4   2
The text of this book is set in 17 pt. ITC Leawood Book.
The illustrations are rendered in watercolors.

Library of Congress Cataloging-in-Publication Data
Lasky, Kathryn.
The solo / by Kathryn Lasky ; illustrations by Bobette McCarthy. — 1st ed.
p.   cm.
Summary: When she is excluded from the group dance, a little girl
insists to her family that she is going to dance a solo at her
school's spring concert—with the entire air force in the audience.
ISBN 0-02-751664-4
[1. Self-reliance—Fiction. 2. Friendship—Fiction. 3. Dancing—
Fiction.] I. McCarthy, Bobette, ill. II. Title.
PZ7.L3274So 1994   [E]—dc20   92-44456

For Kelly and Kristi, with much love
—Aunt B.

Sara Jane won't let me in her dance.

Once I was in it, but she kicked me out.

It happened on the playground. I saw her standing in a circle with the other kids by the jungle gym. She came over and told me. I was too bossy, she said.

I'll show her, I thought. I decided right then to dance
alone. So I went home to practice all by myself—alone.

Wait! Mom says it's not *alone*. It's called *solo*.
So I tell my dad and my brother. I'm going to dance
solo at the spring concert in front of the whole school
and all the teachers…and the air force.

They all say, "The air force is going to be there?!"

Nobody believes me. My dad says, "Grace, you must be mistaken. Not the air force. Maybe it's another group." My mom says, "The air force? Why is the air force coming to your school?"

"They just are. I don't know why."

My brother says, air force or not, he is going to be
absent the day I dance solo in front of the whole
school. Then he says he might leave the state, maybe
the country, even the planet, possibly the universe, and
go to another cosmos. He thinks he's very smart. I
won't miss him.

And I am still going to dance solo.

I get a tape and put it on. This is hard. The music goes too fast and I go too slow.

So I try a few hippety-hops. It speeds things up. Then the music goes slow and I go too fast.

I have to invent more steps to fill
up the space and cover the notes.
Long leaps and slow turns. I
stick out my leg very slowly and
pretend that my arms are wings.
I think about flying.
I think bird thoughts.

I keep trying.

My mom says I have gumption.

My dad says I have guts.

My brother says I'm dumb. Don't I know that there are two hundred people in our school? That's four hundred eyes watching me dance solo. What if I make a mistake? There's a whole big stage up there. It takes a lot of hippety-hops to get across it.

I say I don't care, and it's probably going to be a thousand eyeballs watching me if you count the air force.

My mom sighs and looks worried. She says I'd better start practicing. "Are you sure about the air force?" she asks again. "Absolutely," I say. I twirl, then I fall down. "Don't worry," I say. "I won't do that at the spring concert." It's hard trying to answer questions and dance at the same time.

My brother says, "You should think about this, Grace:
The whole air force might see you fall down."
"They won't be talking to me, asking me questions
while I'm trying to dance," I say over my shoulder
while I am spinning.
"She needs to practice," my mom says.

I need a costume, too. I go up to the attic, to the box
where we keep dress-up clothes. I find something
sparkly from my grandmother and I find something
with feathers from my great-grandmother. The
feathers will make me look floaty. Maybe a crown, too?
I wonder if it will stay on during the hippety-hops.

My mom's old Spanish shawl with the fringe will make a perfect skirt to shake and shimmer when I twirl. I put it all on: my grandma's feathers and sparkles, my mom's fringe shawl, and somebody's old crown.

Dress rehearsal time.

I float, I shimmer, I shake. The crown falls off but I catch it just in time.

My dad nods. "She's got gumption, all right."

I keep practicing. One two three four…twirl once, twice. I'm thinking about gumption. It sounds like fat gumdrops.

One…two…three…four.

The phone rings. It wrecks my timing. I fall down again.

"It's for you, Grace," Mom says.

"You mean it, Sara Jane?…What do you mean, bossy?
Who, me?…Yeah…okay…bye."
I hang up the telephone. My mom, my brother, and my
dad crowd around me.
"I'm back in the group."

"You mean you're not going to dance solo?" my brother asks.

"Nope, but the air force will still be there."

"Grace, you've got gumption," my dad says.

"Nuts with guts," my brother says.

"You still need to practice," says my mom.